Disney · PIXAR
FINDING NEMO
FISH SCHOOL

By Seymour Mackerel

Illustrated by Philip Hom, Hom & Hom Illustration, and John Loter

Designed by Disney's Global Design Group

Random House 🏠 New York
A Random House PICTUREBACK® Shape Book

Copyright © 2003 Disney Enterprises, Inc./Pixar Animation Studios. All rights reserved under International and Pan-American Copyright Conventions. Published in the United States by Random House Children's Books, a division of Random House, Inc., New York, and simultaneously in Canada by Random House of Canada Limited, Toronto, in conjunction with Disney Enterprises, Inc. PICTUREBACK, RANDOM HOUSE, and the Random House colophon are registered trademarks of Random House, Inc. Library of Congress Control Number: 2002113318 ISBN: 0-7364-2127-0

www.randomhouse.com/kids/disney

Printed in the United States of America
20 19 18

emo loved everything about school. He loved swimming there every day with his dad, he loved his classmates, he loved his teachers, and he loved to learn.

And he really loved field trips—even though on his very first trip, he was fish-napped by a scuba-diving dentist and brought to an office aquarium in Sydney.

But that's another story!

Every morning, Nemo's dad, Marlin, would take him to school. Along the way, Nemo always liked to ask his dad lots of questions.

"What is a whale's tongue like, Dad?" Nemo asked.

"Well, it's kind of big and—" Marlin began.

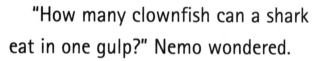

"How many clownfish can a shark eat in one gulp?" Nemo wondered.

"Well, I guess it depends on the size of the—" Marlin started.

"Actually, why are we called clownfish?" Nemo asked.

"You're not funny at all!"

Nemo saw his best friends, Tad, Pearl, and Sheldon.
They loved to play tag and "algae in the middle" before
school started.

Mr. Ray was on schoolyard duty that morning.
He was everyone's favorite teacher. Nemo and his
friends had a special song they made up just for him.

"He's our favorite teacher.
Hip, hip, hooray
For the big, spotted manta.
We love Mr. Ray!"

Then it was time for school to begin. The first class of the day was music, taught by Señor Seaweed. Nemo and his classmates were getting ready for the spring concert. Nemo played the conch shell. Sheldon played the clams. (The clams didn't like it very much!) Tad strummed along on some kelp. And Pearl played sand-dollar tambourines!

Mr. Ray taught science. Today's lesson was
"Your Ocean Home."

Mr. Ray called on Nemo. "Where do you live?"
he asked.

"An enemy, I mean emony, I mean . . . ," said Nemo.

"Nemo lives in an anemone," said Mr. Ray. "While the rest of us would be hurt by its stings, Nemo brushes himself against the anemone every day, so the stings don't bother him."

The rest of the class looked at Nemo in awe.

"That's right!" Nemo said proudly.

Then it was lunchtime!

There were a lot of lunchroom rules. No inking in the lunch area. No throwing worms. No eating your classmates, no matter how tasty they look.

Nemo took out his lunch. "I'll trade you my kelp
sandwich for your algae pizza," he said to Tad.
"Yum!" said Tad.

After lunch was recess. Yay! Everyone had fun
playing hide-and-seek, but then Sandy Plankton got into
a bit of trouble.

"It's like my dad always says," said Nemo. "It's all fun
and games until someone gets stuck in a giant clam."

Once Sandy was free, it was time for Nemo's next class.
It turned out that there was a guest teacher that day—Dory!
"Hi, Elmo!" she cried, waving to Nemo.
Dory was teaching the class how to speak whale.

"Repeat after me," she instructed. *"Eeyouurbawlla kaava. Pwonk! Pwonk! Frooooomaafkapleweyoo."*

"What did you say?" the class asked eagerly.

"I just said hello!" Dory exclaimed.

Then it was show-and-tell time. Pearl brought in a cool piece of coral she had found. And Sheldon, the sea horse, had some big news—his dad was having babies!

"Who wants to go next?" asked Mr. Hermit.

Nemo raised his fin. "Today I have some very special visitors for you all to meet. Come right in, guys."

Anchor, Bruce, and Chum swam in. "Pleased to meetcha," said Chum. "Don't worry, kids, we don't eat fish anymore. Well, we try not to anyway."

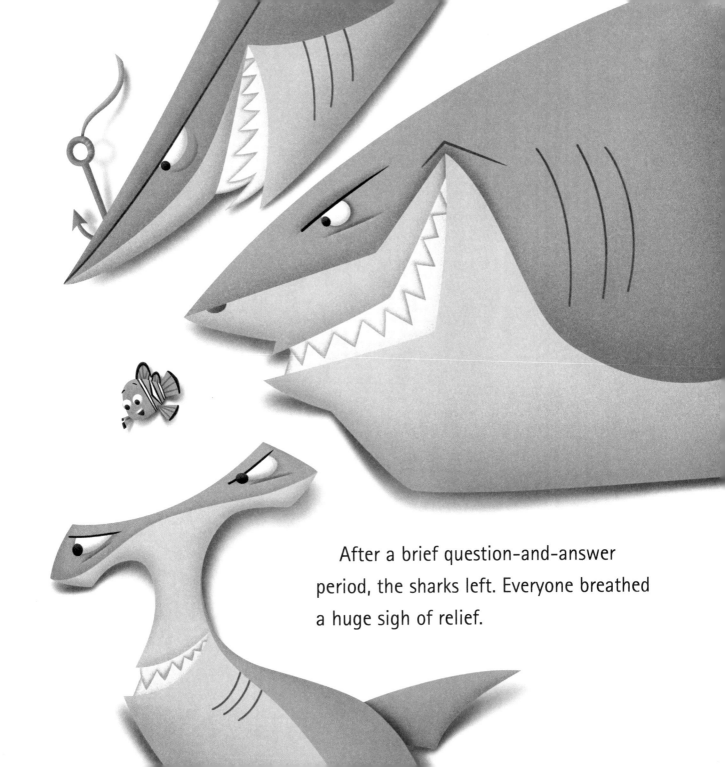

After a brief question-and-answer
period, the sharks left. Everyone breathed
a huge sigh of relief.

All too soon, it was time to go home. The students filed into the schoolyard to wait for their parents to pick them up. Nemo couldn't wait to see his dad and tell him about all the fun things that had happened.

They sang the rest of the Mr. Ray song as they waited:

"He's our science teacher.
We think he is swell.
Sometimes we act goofy,
but he never does yell."

"Aw, shucks," said Mr. Ray, looking pleased.

Soon Nemo's dad arrived. "How was your day today, son?" he asked Nemo as they swam home.

"Oh, Dad, it was awesome!" Nemo cried. "Sandy got stuck in a clam, Dory taught whale, and I brought in the sharks for show-and-tell. . . ." He paused to take a breath. "I can't wait till tomorrow!"

Marlin shook his head sadly. "I'm sorry, Nemo, I can't let you go to school tomorrow . . . because . . .

... tomorrow's Saturday!"